The Perfect Dress

By Michael Scotto,
Eric Graf &
Alan Olson

Illustrated By Evette Gabriel,
Dion Williams &
Yukiko Adachi

WELCOME TO MIDLANDIA
OUR STORY BEGINS

HERE

Midlandia University

Community Center

Animal Land

Town Square

Playland Park

Bike Factory

Harvest Farms

Sew was the seamstress for all of Midlandia. She mended clothes that were torn, and she made new clothing, too.

The dress Sew wore was very special. She had taken the leftover bits of cloth from each thing she had ever made and put them together to make something colorful.

Each piece reminded Sew of each person she had helped.

One morning, Builda hurried into Sew's shop. Builda owned a bicycle factory in town, and she was always in a rush. "Good morning, Builda," Sew said. "What brings you here today?"

Builda quickly checked her clipboard. "Well," she replied, "first I cleaned my house from top to bottom. Then I had a quick morning workout with my pal Sensei. And now, I am here because I need a new dress."

Sew was a little puzzled. "But didn't I make you a new dress just last month?" "Well, yes," Builda said. "But that dress was for a dinner party, and now I'm going to a dinner dance. **I need something new.**"

"**Okay...**" Sew said as she took a measurement. "If you insist. What kind of dress would you like?" "I want it exactly like the last one," Builda said. "Only, put some pink ruffles on the sleeves this time."

"Come back in a week," Sew said, "and your dress will be ready."

Builda checked her list. "Oh my!" she cried.
"I wasted all this time talking to you, and
now I'm going to be late to the factory!"
And with that, Builda dashed off.

Sew **worked** and **cut** and **stitched** for a whole week,
until she thought Builda's new dress was perfect.

But when Builda returned....

"I don't like it!" Builda shouted. "Maybe you like wearing shabby rags, but I can't bear it."

"What do you mean?" Sew asked. "All I mean," Builda said, "is that I am a stylish Midlandian, and I can't be seen wearing the kind of clothes that you wear. **Okay?"**

Sew didn't quite know what to say, so she just nodded her head. "I'll be back for my new dress tomorrow," Builda said. **"And it had better be perfect!"**

Sew didn't know much about fancy clothes, but she knew she could learn about them at the library.

"You're here late," Dewey said. Dewey was a librarian. He helped all the Midlandians who came to the library find what they needed. "Do you have any books on fancy dresses?" Sew asked.

Dewey helped Sew find lots of books full of pretty dresses. "But I have no idea which one is perfect!" Sew thought. She became very worried. "Are you all right, Sew?" Dewey asked.

"I just don't know what to do!" Sew moaned. "Builda wants the perfect dress, but I don't know if I can cut it!"

"But Sew, everyone loves your clothes," Dewey said. "Why are you worried?"

Sew hung her head. "Builda said that my dress
was a bunch of shabby rags," she whispered.

"That was not a nice thing for her to say," Dewey told her. "It's okay if Builda does not like the clothes that you wear, but she should not tease you about them. The important thing is that your clothes are perfect for you."

"You're right, Dewey," Sew said. "I feel a little better."
"That's what the D-Man is here for!" he replied.

Sew worked through the night, but it was just not enough time to finish a whole new dress. In the morning, Builda rushed into Sew's shop. "Where is my dress?" Builda demanded.

"One day wasn't
enough time to finish it,"
Sew said. "I can show
you what I have."

When Builda saw the dress,
she turned bright red! "Maybe you
like wearing half a dress," she cried,
"but I need a whole one!"

Sew had had enough! "The way you are talking to me isn't very nice," she said. "If you can't start being nice, I can't finish your dress for you."

Builda was stunned. **"What do you mean?"** she asked. **"I'm very nice."**

"**No**," Sew replied. "You were not nice yesterday when you said my dress was shabby." "**But look at it**," Builda said. "**It's just a bunch of scraps.**"

"It might look like a bunch of scraps to you," Sew said, "but each piece means something to me. Every time I make new clothes, I save a little piece of the cloth and add it to my dress. That way, I never forget all the people I've helped."

Sew showed Builda a little square at the bottom of her dress. "This is from the dress I made for you last month. You might not think that it's fancy enough, but every scrap is special to me."

"I didn't realize what your dress meant to you," Builda said. "But now that I know, **I'm really sorry for calling it shabby.** And I'd love it if you would come with me to the dinner dance and wear it there."

"I'd love to!" Sew said.

The next evening, the two friends went together to the dance, and everybody admired Sew's handiwork. The two dresses were very different, but each one was a perfect fit.

Discussion Questions

Which dress did you like better, Builda's or Sew's? Why?

In the story, was Builda a bully? Why was she wrong?

What should you do if someone bullies you?

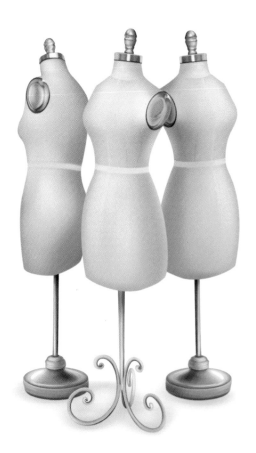